The Curse of the Jelly Babies

The Curse of the Jelly Babies

YOU, me and Thing

Karen McCombie

ff

faber and faber

First published in 2011
by Faber and Faber Limited
Bloomsbury House,
74–77 Great Russell Street,
London, WC1B 3DA

Printed in England by CPI Bookmarque, Croydon

A CIP record for this book
is available from the British Library

ISBN 978–0–571–27239–6

2 4 6 8 10 9 7 5 3 1

For Alice Mary Brown,
with love and huggles

Contents

Once upon a Thing . . .

I never expected to be friends with a Thing.

Well, you don't, do you?

You usually think of friends being either boys or girls, or maybe even cute yappy dogs or something.

Well, Thing certainly doesn't fit into any of *those* categories.

Thing is just a . . . a . . .

Actually, I'm not sure quite *how* to

describe it.

'A sort of troll crossed with a fairy crossed with a squirrel?' Jackson suggested, after we first discovered Thing.

'I is *not* a squirrel,' Thing purred grumpily at the time, twitching its squirrelly ears at Jackson. 'And not a fairy or a trolly. Whatever they is.'

By the way, I never expected to be friends with Jackson Miller either.

I guess I've got a bit of explaining to do, about Jackson and about Thing.

(Oh, and about curses and jelly babies too, I suppose. *And* the magic. I mustn't forget the magic!)

But how do I start?

Well, I *could* do it with a once-upon-a-time . . .

That's the way an awful lot of stories start, I know. But I'm Ruby Morgan, and I've never begun a story with a once-upon-a-time ever before in my entire life (which has lasted nine years so far) and I'd quite like to give it a try, if nobody minds.

So, are you ready? Here goes . . .

Once upon a time, a girl called Ruby (that's me!) lived with her parents in a very old cottage at the edge of small town.

The cottage had roses round the door, a nicely tangly front garden where an old cat called Christine liked to snooze, a little windy road that meandered to the town, and a view of a few swishy-swashy fields of hay.

At the back of the house was another, bigger, nicely tangly

garden, and beyond that were trees, trees, trees and quite a lot more trees. To Ruby, it seemed like Muir Wood went on forever (just about). It was packed full of fat cooing wood pigeons boinging around on skinny twiglets, and delicious smells of pinecones and damp leafness. There were acres of old roots and branches and lots of rustly stuff which were perfect to make dens in, if you were Ruby.

(By the way, that's the good part of this once-upon-a-time bit of my story – the bad news part is coming right up.)

Ruby didn't pay much attention to her parents frowning at reports in the local newspapers and tutting to each other in corners when they thought she wasn't listening.

But she did take quite a **LOT** of notice when a bunch of diggers and lorries came barrelling down the windy road outside her house. And she took a whole **HEAP** of notice when gaggles of guys in yellow safety helmets and stern boots started stomping through the woods, hacking through just about every tree they came across with their buzzing big chainsaws.

(See? I warned you that bit was bad news.)

And so – like this once-upon-a-time story explains – my cottage used to sit happily on the edge of Muir Wood.

Then it turned into the odd-one-out amongst a whole Legoland of shiny brand-new houses called the 'Forest View Estate'.

Ha!

Apart from the five trees at the end of our

FOREST VIEW ESTATE ✿

garden, there wasn't a forest left to have a view of!

OK, so now you know how it was, and how it is.

What shall I tell you about next?

Thing? Jackson? The curse? Or the jelly babies? (I haven't forgotten about the magic, I promise!)

I guess it's got to be Jackson, 'cause he came first.

Though at the time, I wished he hadn't come at all ...

2

Funny feelings and *ffftts!!*

It couldn't get any worse.

(Actually, it could.)

Having a pile of boring brick houses dumped on top of a lovely wood was bad enough.

But having one built slap-bang next door to us was terrible, because . . .

a) it was slap-bang next door to us

b) a two-hundred-year-old oak tree got cut down and dug up to make room for it

c) the new house's back garden was made up of ugly paving stones and pebbles where there should be pretty green things and flowery bits, obviously

d) the new house's **FRONT** garden had two large cars, a bright red bike and a skateboard where there should be roses and snoozing cats

e) all I could see from my bedroom window at the side of my house was the bedroom window at the side of **THAT** house.

Now e) was a
MAJOR problem.

Here's why . . . the
bedroom opposite mine
belonged to a boy
who I instantly liked as
much as nettlerash.

Get this: one
morning, I woke up – as usual – with
Christine cat purr-urr-urring in my ear.

And – as usual – I pulled my curtains
wide open to get a view of the sky and what
it was doing.

But instead of a view of the sky, or even
the branches of the lovely old oak that used
to stand there, I found myself gawping at
a boy.

A boy with blond hair, who was howling
along to a loud hip-hop song while picking
his *nose*.

And – get this – he was only wearing *boxer shorts*!

It gets even worse.

The boy caught sight of me, and instead of acting embarrassed, he grinned like a crazy baboon, then turned round and wiggled his bum!

Shocked, I clung on to the curtains, stared at my revolting new neighbour, and missed the tree very, very badly. It was a lot quieter and had *much* better manners.

A little bit later that morning, I went to school with a black cloud of gloom floating invisibly above my head.

'Ah, here she comes now!' my teacher Miss Wilson said cheerfully, as I wandered into class.

Beside her was a boy I'd only seen once before.

(Can you guess who?)

He had scruffy blond hair, a grin like a baboon and was wearing considerably more clothes than he had been earlier.

'Jackson, this is your new neighbour!' trilled Miss Wilson. 'Ruby—'

FffTT!!

My teacher hesitated at the small,

sort of *farty* noise we'd all just heard. Then she continued, probably just assuming that the noise was the squeak of a chair.

'Ruby—'

Ffftt!!

'Ruby lives in the old cottage next door to your new house, Jackson,' Miss Wilson continued, with a slightly confused frown. 'Don't you, Ruby?'

Ffftt!!

Miss Wilson glanced around to find out where the nearby noise was coming from. Jackson did the same thing, frowning too.

'Um, right – we'll put you at the empty space on that table next to her, Jackson,' she finally carried on, a little flustered by the odd noises. 'That way, you can be neighbours in the classroom too!'

Around me, boys and girls were sitting down, all ready for the register. One by one,

they muttered a 'Yes, miss!' as Miss Wilson
called their names out.

'Jackson Miller!'

'**YES, MISS!**' Jackson bellowed, which
made everyone but me laugh.

(*I* was too busy realising he was also my
neighbour on the class register, worse luck.)

'Ruby Morgan?'

Ffftt!! came the stupid noise again, and
giggles erupted around the room.

OK – that was IT!

I suddenly knew for sure who was making
that noise, even if Miss Wilson didn't. I fumed
all the way to breaktime then stomped *right*
up to Jackson Miller in the playground.

As soon as he saw me coming he did his
baboon grin and slid his right hand under
his left arm.

'Are you going to make that stupid noise
every time you hear my name?' I demanded.

'Probably! Why — does it bug you, Ruby?' he asked, while squelching a big fat *Ffftt!!* with his hand and his armpit.

I didn't bother to answer him.

With that one dumb sound, I vowed that I would never, ever in a *million years* be friends with a donut like Jackson Miller!

Oops.

My vow broke *long* before I got to a million years.

It broke by about half-past four that afternoon, thanks to a little thing called, er, Thing . . .

3

Phew and hurray

Some people are born to be smart.

Some are born to be caring.

And some people – like Jackson Miller – are born to be annoying, as you are about to see (and hear) . . .

Thud! Thud! Thudda-dudda-dudda!
Thudda-dudda-dudda!
Thud! Thud! Thudda-du
Thudda-dudda-du

Blaring from next door was some very loud music.

It woke up Christine cat, who'd just settled down for a snoozle amongst the daisies and dandelions on our lawn.

It almost completely drowned out the gentle tweetly-tweeting of the birds in the huddle of trees at the bottom of my garden.

That was a real shame because

the tweetly-tweeting had been keeping me company while I was hanging out some washing for Mum.

The tweetly-tweeting had been putting me in a good mood, after a tiring day avoiding Jackson Miller and his stupid armpit trick.

And now it sounded as if he was turning his back garden into a drum 'n' bass nightclub.

ARRGHH!!!

Pegging up the last piece of washing, I was all set to stomp over to the fence that separated us. I planned to tell Jackson Miller *just* what I thought of him and his music.

But he beat me to it, because – like I mentioned – he was born to be annoying.

'Hey, *NICE PANTS!*' Jackson bellowed.

I looked over and saw him leaning his elbows on the top of the fence, grinning like the big baboon he was.

Ping!

I yanked the pants off the washing line and stuffed them damply in my jeans pocket. (They were pale blue, with daisies, if you wanted to know. But you probably didn't.)

'Go away, Jackson,' I muttered.

'OK!' said Jackson. And with that, he took one cheeky, doll-size step back.

Grinding my teeth together, I unhooked the peg bag from the line and ignored him.

'Hey, Ruby, can I ask you something?'

Jackson suddenly said, while waving a remote control in the direction of his house. (Phew – it turned the loud music off. And hurray – he'd forgotten to make the farty noise when he said my name.)

'NO!' I growled, certain that Jackson's question was going to be an annoying or useless one like 'Would you like to smell my socks?'

'I was wondering, is there anything to *do* round here?' Jackson asked, ignoring my no *and* my growling. 'This place seems to be a bit, well, *boring* . . .'

As he spoke, Jackson chucked something yellow up in the air and casually caught it in his mouth.

I was pretty sure it was a jelly baby.

I hoped it would choke him.

'It didn't *used* to be boring! There was a HUGE wood right *there*,' I snapped, pointing to the clump of trees just over the back of my stone garden wall. Somehow the builders had forgotten to cut those last few down. 'And you could walk through it and have adventures in it *all* day!'

'Really?' said Jackson, wrinkling his nose as if he didn't quite believe me. 'Where did it go?'

(OK, so some people are born to be annoying – AND stupid.)

'The wood got chopped down and went to the timber yard,' I said sharply. 'Then *your* house and all these *other* houses got built where it stood!'

'Wow,' Jackson muttered.

It was tricky to tell what he was thinking.

Maybe he was quietly shocked to hear about the damage his home had done to the environment.

Or maybe he was just wondering whether

to have another jelly baby or not.

'And it's not just the *trees* that are gone, you know!' I carried on, hoping I might make him understand. 'Lots of wildlife lived there too.'

'Right!' he mused, like he was getting it at last. 'So what, uh, happened to all the animals?'

'The developers built them a little petting zoo to live in,' I lied.

'Wow? *Did* they?'

(See? What did I say about him being annoying AND stupid?!)

'Of *course* they didn't!' I sighed. Good grief, it was like explaining multiplication to a *frog*.

I immediately thought of the deer and rabbits and teeny-weeny voles and stuff that had to flee when the diggers and cement mixers and chainsaws moved in.

They'd have had to cross fields and rivers

and dual carriageways to find new habitats, running the risk of starvation or being squished on busy roads. It was all *way* too tragic . . .

'Hey, wanna jelly baby?' Jackson suddenly asked, while tossing a black one in the air and catching it in his mouth.

'ARRGHH!' I roared. Jackson Miller was SO infuriating!!

'Just say "Yes, please", or "No, thank you", Ruby!' he said, with a maddening baboon grin.

I was on the point of losing my temper and throwing the first thing I could find at him. (Luckily I didn't – it might have been my pants.)

27

But suddenly Jackson stopped grinning.

'Can you hear that?' he asked, sticking a finger in the air.

'Yes!' I said snippily. '*Obviously* I can hear you chewing – you've got your mouth open!!'

'No – not *that*!' Jackson replied, tilting his head to listen better.

Silence.

Sort of.

'I meant *that* . . .'

Hardly daring to breathe, I froze and listened to the minuscule noises.

'Peh!' **Zhush –swizh –zhush**. 'Peh!'

'That' seemed to be the sound of rustling and sighing. And it was coming from the direction of the trees.

'Could be a hedgehog, tangled up in something?' I murmured to Jackson.

Mirroring each other, we softly padded

down our gardens. At the end of mine was a low stone wall. At the end of Jackson's was a tall fence he'd have to stand on tiptoe to see over.

And so together we peered (high and low) and saw . . . (hold your breath . . .)

A plastic Tesco shopping bag.

Snarled up with some sticks.

And it was **trembling**.

'Do you still think it's a hedgehog?' Jackson whispered to me.

Whatever it was, it *knew* we were staring at it, that was for sure. All the **zhush-swizh-zhush**-ing and 'peh!'-ing had stopped.

'I don't know,' I mumbled, my heart thumpety-thumping as I hoicked my leg over the wall and plopped on to the mossy grass at the foot of the trees.

Jackson followed, hurling himself over his tall fence and landing with a jarring thump.

The snarled-up Tesco-bag-and-sticks thing
jerked in alarm.

And uh-oh, through a rip in the plastic, I
could make out a tiny snout and a pair of
round, panicked eyes.

'There, there . . .' I said in a soft voice, as I
hunkered down beside the trapped whatever-
it-was. 'Do you need some help, little guy?'

'Yes, *please*,' came a strange, *purring* sort of
voice from inside the bag-and-twig tangle.

'Ooh!' I squeaked in shock.

'Oof!' grunted Jackson, as he flew back in surprise, banging his head on the fencepost.

With a *whoosh*, a small paw/hand reached out from another rip in the bag, and patted the toe of Jackson's trainer.

'Ouchy! There, *there* . . .' said the thing inside the bag.

Well, whatever the weird, talking alien creature was, at least it seemed quite kind.

I just hoped it would be as kind to *me*, because all of a sudden my head was going swirly . . .

and I felt like I was . . .

about to · · ·

A sweet squish

I woke up with something being squished in my ear.

'*No* . . . that's not going to help!' I heard Jackson say.

'But look – I press it in, and girly's eyes *open*!' said the small, purry voice.

I winced as the squashy something got squished in my ear again.

'Probably because it feels a bit weird. Jelly babies are for *mouths*, not for ears,' Jackson explained to whatever it was.

Next, I saw him leaning over me.

'Are you OK, Ruby? I think you fainted.'

At the same time as Jackson spoke, a pointy little finger poked me in the ribs and the purry little voice said, 'Girly forgot to breathe. Got to *breathe*, girly!'

'But I *was* breathing!' I protested, unplugging the jelly baby from my ear and sitting up woozily.

Then I remembered . . .

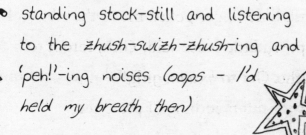

- standing stock-still and listening to the *zhush-swizh-zhush*-ing and 'peh!'-ing noises (*oops – I'd held my breath then*)

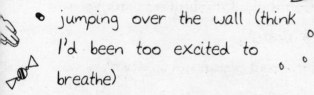

- jumping over the wall (*think I'd been too excited to breathe*)

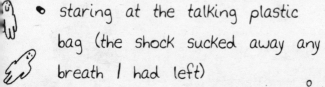

- staring at the talking plastic bag (*the shock sucked away any breath I had left*)

So yep, it looked like I had fainted.

How nuts was that?

Speaking of nuts, what about that talking plastic bag ...

'EEK!' I squeaked, suddenly noticing the furry, gingery thing by my side.

It was the size of a squirrel, but apart from the ears, didn't look much like one.

'EEK!' squeaked the non-squirrel, as panicked as me.

At least, I was pretty *sure* it wasn't a squirrel. In all the years I'd wandered the woods, I'd never seen a squirrel that looked like *this*. It had huge, scaredy, bushbaby eyes, and a face that seemed almost human, except for the wet black snout.

Then there were the paws with furry fingers, and . . . and . . . wings!

Stubby, bumpy *wings*, tucked neatly at its back!

It was like a science experiment gone very, oddly *wrong* . . .

'Is it an alien?' I asked Jackson, my heart immediately thumpety-thumping again (*remember to breathe, remember to breathe*, I ordered myself).

'What is a Nalien?' the thing asked Jackson, nervously folding its little paws together in front of its fluffy chest.

'Something from another planet,' Jackson explained, looking remarkably calm for someone speaking to a possible Nalien.

'What is a Nuther Planet?' the thing asked Jackson.

'Like Earth, only in outer space!' Jackson said all enthusiastically, as if he was talking to some human buddy.

'What is Nouter—'

'Look, where do you come from?' I interrupted the thing, with a more simple question.

This useless conversation with the mystery creature was already starting to go round in so many circles it could tie us all up in knots.

'Over *there*,' it purred, pointing in the direction of the horrible, dull houses beyond the trees.

'Willow Avenue?!' I muttered, reading the road sign that was just visible through the foliage and shrubs.

Huh?

Was the thing some kind of deluxe, remote-controlled robotic toy, belonging to a kid who lived there?

'No, thank you,' said the thing, wobbling from side to side and moving towards me. 'I come from long, long, long way inside woods. Long, long, long, long, *long* way inside.'

I looked at the small thing with its huge, scaredy eyes and felt instantly sorry for it.

It was no robot.

It was a living, breathing, er, *thing*, and whatever it was, it had lost its habitat, same as the deer and the rabbits and the teeny-tiny voles and stuff.

'Had you lived there for a long time?' I asked gently.

I was slightly unnerved at how close it was standing to me and how hard its bushbaby eyes were staring at the side of my head.

'A long, long, long time. A long, long, long, long, *long* time,' it muttered, reaching a paw out towards me.

'You had to leave your home behind when the men came with the chainsaws, didn't you?' I said, picturing the little creature scampering away in fear as the noise of men and machinery and crashing trees filled its ears.

'Yes, please,' said the thing, suddenly flicking my earlobe back and forth with its finger. 'What is *this*?'

'It's part of my ear!' I told it, moving back out of flicking distance.

'It's floppy. *Nice*,' the thing said with a crooked smile of wonderment.

'Hey!' Jackson suddenly blurted out. 'This bag I unwrapped you from – was this a sort of tent?'

'What is a Sortoftent?'

'I mean, were you living in it, or under it?' I said quickly, before we got in a confusing looped conversation again.

'Yes, please,' nodded the thing, wobbling side-to-side. 'But it is not a *good* house. I like my *old* house. Wish I still in old house. I build it nice. All branches and twigs. *Crunchy.*'

I had no idea what that meant. Neither did Jackson, from the frown he just gave me.

But there were other, more important questions that needed to be asked. I was sure we could wait to find out what a crunchy house looked like.

'What *are* you?' I asked bluntly.

'Not know,' it answered, giving up on my earlobe and now turning to twiddle the metal button on the waistband of my jeans as if it was a mini steering wheel. 'What are *you*?'

'We're humans,' I explained. 'My name is Ruby—'

Out of the corner of my eye, I saw Jackson automatically raise his right hand towards his left armpit and gave him a don't-you-dare glare.

'—and this is Jackson. We live in those two buildings behind us. Do you have a name?'

'No, thank you,' purred the thing, hooking a finger in my belt loop and tugging quite hard for something so small.

(I felt like I was being explored. It was kind of cool to be so interesting, but I wished it would go and explore Jackson instead . . .)

'Are there any more of you? Did you have a family before the builders came?' I asked, rocking back and forward a little as the thing tugged.

'No, thank you. *Always* me only.'

'How can you speak? Our language, I mean?' said Jackson, asking a sensible and important question for once.

'I hear people walk and talk in the woods,' explained the thing. 'I hide but I listen and *learn*.'

'You've learned very well,' I praised it, wondering if it had ever heard me and my parents or friends yakking over the years. (How weird would *that* be?)

'Your language *hard*,' it continued. 'Starling is harder. Very big complicated. Snail is easy.'

'What? You can speak *snail*!' Jackson said incredulously. 'Go on then, say something in snail!'

The thing blinked a bit, then opened its mouth.

'   ?'

'I couldn't hear anything!' I told it.

'*That* how loud snails speak,' the thing said simply.

'So can you try again at *human* volume?' I suggested.

The thing hesitated, then made a slurping sound.

'Cool! What did that mean?' Jackson asked.

'*Eat*,' answered the thing.

'Can you say something else in snail?'

The thing shrugged at Jackson. 'There is twenty-seven *more* words in snail language, but they will all sound same *way* to you.'

'Really? So what do the other twenty-seven words translate as?' I asked.

'*Eat.* All just mean *Eat*,' explained the thing.

'TEA'S READY!' I suddenly heard Mum call out. 'WHERE ARE YOU, RUBY?'

I looked in a panic at Jackson; the idea of the small whatever-it-was being all alone and homeless was awful, however useless its home was.

Jackson seemed to understand.

'It's fine – you go,' he told me, as he fumbled with the tent. 'I'll stay here and fix this!'

'COMING, MUM!' I called out, then turned back to Jackson. 'Maybe see you here later, if I can get back out?'

'Yeah, I'll try too,' Jackson said with a nod and a grin.

As I got to my feet and leapt back over the wall, he lifted a hand and waved.

'But listen, Ruby,' he called out before I vanished, 'don't tell anyone about . . . *this*, OK?! Let's talk more about it first, yeah?'

'All right.' I nodded uncertainly, as I walked backwards.

And as I walked, I saw the thing studying Jackson – then it began to copy him and wave at me too.

With a pair of still-damp, daisy-print pants clutched in its paw.

ARRGHH . . .!!

5
Talking without speaking

Tea got in the way.

Then homework.

Then Gran phoned for ages.

So I never did make it back out to the garden and the thing last night.

Same went for this morning.

After tossing and turning and dreaming of small things all night, I woke up at ten-to-eek!-I'm-late!, and had three-quarters-of-a-nano-second to have breakfast and get ready for school.

And now it was twenty-past nine and I was sitting in our ICT lesson – with a big, grinning baboon *leering* at me from the computer screen!

OK, so it was the reflection of Jackson, suddenly hovering over my shoulder.

'Jackson Miller! Nice of you to join us!' said Miss Wilson, looking up from someone else's monitor as she spotted him standing behind me, breathless from running. 'The bell went ages ago . . . that's not a great start on your second day, is it?'

'No, Miss Wilson,' muttered Jackson, sliding into the empty seat next to me. 'I got lost.'

PLING! went the on-button of his computer.

FROWN went my forehead, which translated as 'What's up?', 'cause I was pretty

sure Jackson *couldn't* have got lost. School
was the first building you came to when you
followed the windy road into town.

Jackson glanced round to check Miss
Wilson wasn't watching and replied to my
frown with a mime, which went like *this* ...

- he pointed to himself (I decided
  that meant 'I')

- raised a hand above his eyes
  ('looking')

- put his hands up in front of him
  like paws and opened his eyes as
  wide as he could (that was the
  thing, for sure)

He'd been out looking for the thing?
So *that's* why he'd been late!

I raised my eyebrows in reply (translation: 'Did you find it?').

Jackson understood, which was pretty amazing for a boy with a head full of jelly babies.

He nodded, then pointed to his stomach, his open mouth, then made the paws and big, sad eyes mime again.

I tried to think of a mime back, but couldn't, so mouthed, 'It's *hungry*?' at Jackson.

Poor little thing . . .

I didn't know whether it preferred to snack on berries or bugs, but as the houses got built and the woods started shrinking, its

breakfast, lunch and tea options must have started shrinking too, I realised.

Jackson nodded, then pulled out an empty

bag of jelly babies from his
pocket, rustled it and gave me
a thumbs-up.

Big mistake.

(WARNING: If you ever
want to show someone an empty packet
of sweets to let them know you've fed a
starving mysterious talking creature who's
living at the bottom of your garden, DON'T
do it in class in front of your teacher . . .)

'*Thank* you, Jackson!' said Miss Wilson,
swooping out of nowhere and snatching the
bag from his hand. 'Enough with the litter.
Now can you *please* get on with the project?'

'Sorry, Miss Wilson,' muttered Jackson,
swiftly turning to the instruction sheet that
was lying by his keyboard.

As Miss Wilson pit-pattered away, I
quickly faced the screen and carried on with
my own work.

But I was pretty much immediately distracted.

The scritchy-scratchy sound of a frantic pencil made me sneak a peek sideways. What *was* Jackson Miller writing on the back of his instruction sheet?

Shoomf!

I was about to find out – he'd just shoved it across to me.

Flipping the paper over, I read:

We mustn't tell ANYONE about the thing cos adults panic about stuff that is different and they will take it to a zoo or a secret lab or something and they'll stick it in a cage and POKE it and put wires in it and do EXPERIMENTS cos they want to figure out what it is so promise you won't tell!!!!!!!!!!!!!

Wow.

Two thoughts zapped into my head as I read Jackson's note:

- I realised he was right – the thing had lost just about its whole world when the housing estate was built, and it would be totally super-cruel to take it away from the few straggly trees that were left

- Jackson really needed to concentrate more on his punctuation

SWOOP!

Now it was *my* turn to have Miss Wilson snatch something out of my hands.

EEK!!!

'What have we here, Ruby?' she asked, wrinkling her nose up at the sight of major scrawling.

Help, help, help . . . I'd managed to keep the top-secret secret safe for about half a nano-second!

Now Miss Wilson would tell the Headteacher, who'd tell the police, who'd tell some scientists or someone, who'd come and scoop up a frightened thing and take it to who knows where and—

'It's mine!' Jackson bellowed. 'It was a film I watched on DVD last night – I was just describing it to Ruby!'

'Well,' sighed Miss Wilson, flipping the instruction sheet the right way up and tapping it with her finger. 'Save the chit-chat till breaktime, please, Jackson!'

As she turned to go, me and Jackson looked at each other and – in a psychic,

spooky,★ I-can-read-your-mind kind of way
– knew *exactly* what each other was thinking.

And that was a great big,

'*Phew ...*'

★ Speaking of spooky, I promised you magic, didn't I?
Well, it might be just about to happen. (Turn the page
– *quick!*)

6

Seriously spectacular weirdness

OK, so there have been a *few* jelly babies in this story so far, but not enough.

Still, after school that day there was a whole *trail* of them, leading from the huddle of trees, over my garden wall, under Jackson's fence (he dug a thing-sized tunnel specially) and all the way across the garden to his back door.

It had been the only way to tempt the thing inside.

'Not like buildingings . . .' it purred worriedly, as it ate its way along the multicoloured line of jelly babies. 'Buildingings make trees *go*!'

'Yes, but you need to come in the kitchen and figure out what you like to eat,' Jackson insisted, stepping backwards into his house. 'We don't want you to starve!'

Jackson's mum was still at work, and his dad was lovingly washing and waxing his fancy car in the drive, giving us time to sneak inside and raid the fridge.

Earlier – when we'd got home from school – me and Jackson had both smuggled a bunch of nibbles out to the thing's den. Between us, our haul included a piece of peanut-butter-on-toast, a banana, a chipolata, a slice of honey-roast ham, a Dairylea cheese triangle and a slug.

(By the way, the slug came from Jackson's *garden*, not his kitchen, in case you thought his parents made strange shopping lists.)

Creeping out from under its plastic-bag-and-stick tent, the thing spotted the slug, gave it a stroke, then smiled warmly as it oozed off – so we decided there and then that it must be vegetarian.

Next, it spied the food we'd brought and had a dainty gnaw of it all. But it shuddered and made 'peh!'-ing noises at everything except the green jelly baby that Jackson finally held out.

Sadly, a whole load of jelly babies does *not* add up to a balanced diet – for humans or things – so we needed to work out what to feed our thing and *fast*.

Which was why we'd made the tunnel and laid the trail that led here to the back door of Jackson's house.

'Come on! Just a few more steps . . .' he urged it, patting the cool, grey slate of the kitchen floor.

'No, thank you!' the thing replied, staying where it was on the back doorstep, wringing its paws together and wobbling anxiously from side to side.

Its bushbaby eyes blinked in alarm at the dazzling array of shiny white units.

'*I'll* sit here with it – *you* get some food, Jackson,' I suggested, settling myself down beside the trembly little thing.

It scuttled closer to me, scrambling on to

my lap.

'By the way,' said Jackson, grabbing a tray and beginning to dollop random bits of food on it. 'I meant to ask – are you a boy or a girl?'

Jackson was looking in the fridge at the time, but I guessed the question was aimed at the thing, and not *me*.

'He means *you*,' I told it.

'Oh! Ah . . . not know,' replied the thing, picking up my thumb and examining the nail. It gave it a questioning nibble, then mumbled a small 'peh' of disgust.

'So you don't know if you're a boy or a girl, OR what you are?!' laughed Jackson.

At the same time, he gave up on the inside of the fridge and grabbed a box of

Rice Krispies from the top of it, shaking the contents on to the tray alongside an olive, a tomato, a strawberry yoghurt and a potato.

'Well,' Jackson continued, about to say the *first* thing that would annoy our thing. 'Maybe you're some sort of a troll crossed with a fairy crossed with a squirrel?'

The thing stomped its tiny feet on my lap.

'I is *not* a squirrel! And not a fairy or a trolly. Whatever they is. Peh!'

'Well, your ears *are* quite squirrelly . . .' Jackson carried on, coming over and setting the tray down on the tiled floor.

With a twitch of its squirrelly ears, the thing huffily turned its back on both Jackson and the tray of food.

'What?' asked Jackson, not sure how he'd managed to be so annoying. 'What's wrong with squirrels?'

I shrugged a just-leave-it! shrug in

Jackson's direction. Like crunchy houses, we could wait to find out what the problem was.

'*Please* can you try some of this food,' I implored the thing, holding out a Rice Krispie.

The thing shook its head, stubborn as a tiddly toddler.

'Not *want* to, girly,' it said, as it leant sideways and listened instead to my watch. (One of its back legs started thudding in time to the ticking, like a dog scratching mid-air when you tickle its tummy.)

'All right. But listen, my name's *Ruby*, remember. And we should call *you* something.'

'Why?' the thing asked, like I suspected it might.

'Because *everyone* has a name,' said Jackson, ignoring the fact that he was being ignored. 'Even animals must have names for each other, right?'

He pulled a 'Don't they?' face at me and I pulled a '*I* dunno!' one back.

'Well, what about your friends from the forest? What did *they* call you?' I asked the thing, hoping I didn't make it sad, talking about long-lost creatures from Muir Wood.

The thing wobbled its forehead up and down, thinking hard.

'I liked some woodlice once. They *nice*.

But not talk, just scurry,' it said finally. 'And a bat. I like *one* bat, a long, long, long time ago. A long, long, long, long, *long* time ago. *It* have name for me. It call me . . .'

The thing opened its mouth and from somewhere at the back of its throat made a thin, scratchy, *creaking* noise.

Me and Jackson glanced warily at each other, knowing that it was going to be pretty tricky for us to pronounce *that*.

'Hey,' I began, 'would you mind if we called you something that's a bit easier for *humans* to say?'

The thing blinked at me. 'You can call me any name, Rubby.'

'*Ruby*,' I corrected it gently, nudging Jackson in the shin to stop him from sniggering.

'Hey, *I* know!' Jackson suddenly burst out. 'How about we run through a bunch of names, and see which one you like best?'

Knowing the mood Jackson was in, I suspected that the names were going to be pretty *dumb*. And knowing the mood the *thing* was in, I was worried Jackson might annoy it again.

'How about Vince?'

The thing kept on ignoring Jackson and began instead to undo my watchstrap.

'Don't be stupid, Jackson,' I told him.

'Nah, you're right. It has to be something that'd work for a boy *or* a girl,' Jackson mused, as he opened a nearby cupboard and helped himself to a new bag of jelly babies. 'How about Spot?'

The thing did a small 'peh!' under its breath.

'Or Fang?'

I rolled my eyes as Jackson rustled the bag open. (The thing was tapping its tiny claw-nails on the glass of my watchface.)

'Or Fluffy?'

As Jackson sniggered out *another* useless name, he casually selected an orange jelly baby and got ready to toss it in the air.

'Or—'

AARRGHH!' When would Jackson ever shut up? (I could feel the thing trembling with rage in my lap.)

For a second, I toyed with picking up the potato from the tray and tossing it at him.

But in the same instant, a seriously

★*★*SPECTACULAR*★*

piece of weirdness happened . . .

I felt the thing start to shudder more in my lap, and then –

CRACKLE -SPIT -
FIZZZZZZZZ!!

– flickers of light *danced* around the room, as if someone had set off a sparkler, and that sparkler had gone cartwheeling around the kitchen!!!

Then, just as soon as this amazing mini fireworks show started, it *stopped*.

I felt frozen with shock.

(*Remember to breathe – you know what*

happened last time, I told myself.)

'What *was* that?' I asked, my voice squeakily hoarse in surprise.

The thing didn't answer; it was too busy wringing its little paws together nervously.

Jackson didn't answer; he was too busy choking on his orange jelly baby.

Yikes!

I was just about to leap up and *thwack* him on the back, when I stopped dead, 'cause slithering quickly out of Jackson's mouth was . . . a startled *slug*!!

Huh?

'Blah! Puh! *Yee-uwwww*!!' spluttered Jackson, snatching the slug from his lower lip (*SHLURP!*) and depositing it on the grass outside the back door.

'Sorry, sorry, *sorry*!!' I heard the thing muttering.

At first, I didn't get it.

Why had the thing said *sorry*? How could *any* of this — the *crackle-split-fizzzzzzzzzz-ing*, the dancing lights and the shlurpy slug — be *its* fault?

Unless . . .

'Did — did you just *do* something to Jackson's jelly baby?' I asked it warily.

'*Mmm*,' squirmed the thing. 'Was trying to turn it into one of *those* . . . but got it *wrong*.'

It pointed a small hairy finger at a single Rice Krispie.

Well, that definitely *wasn't* what had just slithered out of Jackson's mouth a second ago.

'Did you do some kind of . . . *magic*?'

The thing nodded at my question, its eyes round and worried.

'Pingy things can happen when I feel . . .'

The thing blinked, stuck for the right word.

It blinked some more.

Still not finding the right word, it gritted its tiny sharp teeth, screwed its eyes closed, clenched its weeny fists tight shut and shuddered just like it had a moment before.

'Shy?' Jackson suggested uselessly.

'ARRGHH!?' I suggested more sensibly, since that's how *I* felt when Jackson was going on (and on and *on*) just now.

'Yes, *please*!' the thing smiled in delight, sensing that I understood. 'The *pingy* things happen when I feel ARRGHH!!'

'So you turned my jelly baby into a slug?!' gasped Jackson in wonder. '*Wow*!'

Bless him, Jackson really is a bit stupid.

Who else would be impressed that they'd had a mean magic trick played on them?

Uh-oh . . . the front door just slammed.

'JACKSON! ARE YOU AROUND? CAN YOU GIVE ME A HAND GETTING

ANOTHER BUCKET OF WATER?'
boomed a voice, as confident footsteps
stomped towards the kitchen.

'Quick! Come here, Thing!' I muttered,
scooping up the trembly creature and
stuffing it inside my hoodie.

(Oops – in the muddle of the panic I'd
accidentally given it a name!)

VOOSH went the zip, across went my arms,
so as soon as Mr Miller came striding into the
kitchen, all he saw was me and Jackson, sitting
on the back step with our strange picnic of
Rice Krispies and raw potato.

'Oh, hello!' Mr Miller boomed at me. 'You
must be Ruby!'

I shot a look at Jackson – to make sure
he wasn't about to do one of his childish
ffftt! noises at the mention of my name –
but he seemed too stunned to do anything,
including talk to his dad.

'Um, yes, that's me. Hello!' I muttered shyly to Mr Miller, at the same time feeling Thing's heart beat *madly* against my chest.

Mr Miller didn't seem to notice how silent his son was being or how weirdly false Jackson's baboon grin was.

Instead he plunged a soapy bucket in the sink and began talking to little old me (EEK!) while slooshing on the tap.

Y'know, maybe what Mr Miller was saying was terribly kind and friendly and interesting, but I wasn't really paying attention (oops, and sorry for being so rude).

'. . . Jackson BLAH BLAH BLAH last school BLAH BLAH BLAH his mother and me BLAH BLAH BLAH new friends BLAH BLAH BLAH . . .'

Here's the reason I wasn't paying attention: while Mr Miller droned on, I felt a wriggle and squiggle happening in the depths of my hoodie.

I wriggled and squiggled a bit myself
so Mr Miller wouldn't notice that a small,
walking, talking creature with magical
powers was burrowing its way out of the

bottom of my top and scampering off at top
speed across the Jacksons' garden.

As it wriggled into the tunnel under the
fence, I saw it turn and peek back at me
with its bushbaby eyes.

'Bye, Rubby!' I saw it mouth at me.

Bye, Thing! I said silently in my head,
giving it the tiniest of secret farewell smiles.

'BLAH, BLAH, BLAH, BLAH?' I suddenly heard Mr Miller say.

Whipping my head and my smile around, I looked at Mr Miller and then at Jackson, hoping my friend would give me a clue about what question his dad had just asked.

'So, which of these IS your favourite food, Ruby?' Jackson translated for me, sweeping his hand over the rubbish picnic selection.

'Oh! Um, this one, actually!' I answered, picking up the first thing that came to hand and taking a big bite.

Of raw potato.

Mmm.

(The things you do for a thing called Thing . . .)

7

The sudden
SPLAT!

So the thing had a name at last, thanks to
the muddle of the panic.

(Thing was the *perfect* name for a thing,
don't you think?)

And when Thing felt *ARRGHH!!* . . . well,
all sorts of strangeness might happen.

(*Crackle-spit-fizzzzzzzzz!!*-ing and
splashes of magic!)

I was lying in bed that night thinking
random thoughts (about Thing, *crackle-*

spit-fizzzzzzzzz!!-ing, dancing lights and
startled slugs) when there was a sudden
SPLAT! at my window.

'Mew?!' said Christine cat, waking up
from her snooze in my sock drawer.

'I don't know either!' I told her, flipping my
duvet back and hurrying over to the window.

I felt very, very EEK!, to be honest, but
then again I couldn't bear not to know what
exactly had splatted.

So I yanked open my curtains, and saw . . .
Thing!!

It was stretched star-shaped on the
windowpane, its little nails scrabbling hard to
get a grip on the glass. (It had *no* chance.)

PLOP!

It landed in a rumpled pile on the window
ledge.

Quickly, I yanked open the window.

'Are you OK?' I asked it.

'Hard air not *nice* . . .' it mumbled, pushing itself upright and tapping on the glass pane with a little finger.

'Ah, yes, glass can be a bit . . . um . . . confusing!' I said, caught between feeling sorry for Thing and trying not to giggle.

'What is confuzzing?' asked Thing, blinking at me and rubbing its tiny paws together.

'Sort of strange,' I explained. 'And it's very

strange to see *you* here. How did you get up
to this ledge? Did you *fly*?'

Thing's stumpy wings didn't look like
they'd lift it a centimetre off the ground,
never mind get it as high as the first floor of
our cottage.

'I climb up *tangle*-vine,' Thing explained,
pointing to the wisteria that was all over
this side of my house. 'Seen *boy's* buildinging.
Now wanted to see *your* buildinging, Rubby.'

'*Ruby*,' I corrected it. 'But how did you
know which room was mine?'

'A bee told me.'

Thing said it simply, its eyes darting
around the room.

'A *bee*?' I blinked at it, trying to imagine
a conversation between a thing and a bee,
which made me go a bit dizzy, actually.

'*Mmm*,' purred Thing. 'Saw it flying around
your buildinging when sun was sunny. Then

it came by trees and I asked where is *you*.
It said this place up *here*. So I came when
moon is moony.'

Aw.

Thing seemed *so* keen to know more
about me and Jackson.

OK, so maybe it was keen to know about
only *me* tonight.

How sweet and cute was *that*?

So sweet and cute I could just—

'What is knobbles in legs, Rubby?'

Knobbles?

In *legs*?

What was the thing *on* about?

I looked at where it was pointing, which
was somewhere a little below where my
nightie ended.

'They're my *knees*,' I told it, realising how
very big and truly *knobbly* human knees are,
when you think about it.

For a second, I thought about comparing them to *Thing's* knees, except they were hidden in a fuzz of ginger fur.

Whatever, Thing seemed to have gotten bored with the knobbles in my legs already.

'And what is that?' it asked, pointing up now to the ceiling. Or maybe it was the wall.

'What is what?' I asked, my own eyes darting about.

'*That*! All lines come togetherer! *See*?'

'Oh, *right*!' I nodded, figuring out what it meant. 'That is called a *corner*.'

No wonder Thing was puzzled. There aren't too many of those in the middle of forests.

'What does it *do*?' Thing blinked.

Hmm.

I had a feeling that explaining things to, er, Thing might sometimes give me brain strain.

Instead of trying to figure out an answer to Thing's question, I changed the subject quickly.

'Do you want to come in and look around?' I offered.

'No, thank you,' Thing said ever-so-politely. 'I can see from *here*. Do you have little people to eat, Rubby?'

It took a second for my brain to unknot – then I realised it meant jelly babies.

'Er, no. Jackson's the one who's addicted to those!' I smiled, settling myself down on my (knobbly) knees by the window.

'What's zaddicted?' asked Thing, gawping at Christine cat, who'd purr-urr-urred herself back to sleep, now that we'd found the source of the *SPLAT!*.

(Christine is very old, and her hobbies are sleeping, snoozing and dozing.)

'Never mind. Anyway, I don't have any

jelly babies. I just wish we knew what *else* you ate . . .'

'Mushrooms!!' squeaked Thing.

'What? I wish you'd told us that earlier!' I laughed in surprise, leaning my elbow on the windowsill, and remembering the under-fence tunnelling and the fridge-raiding that had gone on at Jackson's after school today.

'Human word was lost in my *head* till now.'

'Oh, OK. Well, if you like mushrooms so much, I can go downstairs and see if we have some in the kitch—'

'No, thank you. Tummy full. Found some stinky ones growing under bush. *Mmmm . . .*'

Right, so I now knew two important things:

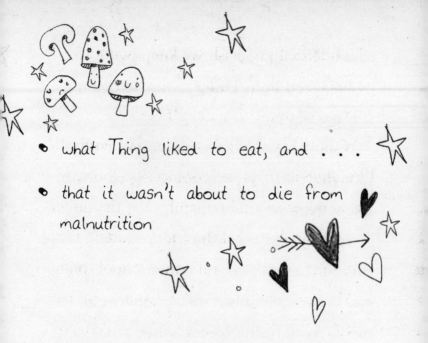

- what Thing liked to eat, and . . .
- that it wasn't about to die from malnutrition

Perhaps it was a good time to find out something *else*.

I was about to ask an important question when a tickly feeling made me giggle instead.

'Hey! Ooo, stop!' I pleaded, as Thing stroked the hairs on my arm as if they were as delicate and fine as the fluff on a dandelion clock.

'Very thin *fur*, girly!' it purred with a

frown. 'Is why you wear wrappings?'

I glanced from Thing to my 'wrappings' (i.e. my nightie).

'I suppose so,' I answered slowly, realising that my 'thin fur' probably made me look like a freak to Thing.

So what did it make of Jackson and *his* thin fur, blond hair and baboon grin? If *I* was a freak, then Jackson must seem like a mega-freak from Nouter Space . . .

Which brought me back to my question.

'Thing . . . what did Jackson do that annoyed you so much today?'

Thing snuffled, and tugged experimentally on one of my arm hairs. Ouch.

'Boy said I was like squirrel. Peh. Then he *ha ha ha* at me, and say names I think not nice . . .'

'Oh, but they weren't *mean* names – just a bit silly!' I said, jumping to Jackson's defence (the big donut). 'He likes fooling around . . .'

'What is foodingaground?'

Oh, good grief . . .

'Something to do with biscuits,' I lied quickly to change the subject (again). 'Anyway, what's so bad about squirrels?'

Thing bristled, and gave its wings a shudder.

(Uh-oh – maybe I shouldn't have asked? I didn't want it to go all *ARRGHH!* again, and end up with slugs up my nose or somewhere unpleasant . . .)

'Squirrels always *ha ha ha* at me and call me not-nice names.'

Right . . . so Jackson had acted like a mean squirrel.

'What sort of not-nice names?' I asked.

Thing thought a bit then made a strange chattery noise – the sort squirrels make when they're chasing each other in swirly circles up tree trunks.

'In *human*, please?' I asked.

'Oh! Uh, "Big-nose-no-tail", and

Phlplplplplp!'

The last name sounded just like someone
blowing a raspberry.

Poor Thing . . . no wonder he wasn't keen
on nasty old squ—

'Why is broken flowers stuck in bottle?'

Thing interrupted my sympathetic thoughts.

It was pointing at my painted jam jar full of bluebells.

'Because they're pretty!' I told it, since *that* was easy to explain. 'Don't you like flowers, Thing?'

'Yes. Always lots of little white one grow round my house after frosty time,' said my small, furry friend, with something like homesickness in its big, glassy eyes. 'But I don't break them and make them *deaded*, Rubby . . .'

Well.

I'd never thought of flowers in a vase that way.

TAPPITY-TAP!!

'Ruby . . . are you talking to yourself in there?' I heard Mum's voice call out to me.

The bedroom door pushed open and the light from the hall gushed in.

'Uh, yes! I mean, no!' I said quickly, resting my head on my hand so that I hid the window ledge as much as possible. 'I mean, I couldn't sleep, so I was looking at the sky, and . . . and singing!'

'Singing what, honey?' Mum smiled at me expectantly.

'Er . . .' I gazed up at the sky and hoped it might give me inspiration. 'It was "Twinkle, Twinkle, Little Star"!'

Urgh.

I hadn't sung that nursery rhyme since I was a kid!

'Oh, honey, that's so *sweet*!' Mum gushed, hurrying over to join me at the window (*don't let her see Thing, don't let her see Thing*). 'I know, let's sing it together, just like when you were little!'

And so, by the light of the silvery moon, my mum and I sang (oh, the shame!) the whole of 'Twinkle Twinkle'.

Meanwhile, outside the window I could make out the faint scrabble of something scurrying through the tangle-vine.

Followed by a faint, purry voice singing down below in the garden.

'*How why wonder watch you are . . .*'

'What was that?' Mum muttered, stopping and listening.

'Just an echo,' I told her, hoping the 'echo' would get back home to its bag-and-twigs home safe and sound . . .

In the blink of a (human) eye

Next day at school, I explained to Jackson that he mustn't be mean as a squirrel.

It took the whole of breaktime to get him to stop laughing and doing mean squirrel impersonations. (He looked more like a zombie rabbit.)

'It's not funny!' I kept saying. 'Thing was really upset with you!'

But it was difficult to get the words out,

since (annoyingly) I'd caught the giggles from Jackson.

Still, annoying or not, Jackson and me were here together after school, hunkered down with Thing in the trees, staring at the lopsided Tesco-bag-and-twig-tent.

'Thing – your home is rubbish. You need a new one,' said Jackson, attempting to push the tent up straight with his finger (it just sagged down again as soon as a passing butterfly happened to land on it). 'Don't you think so, Ruby?'

It was hard to concentrate on what

Jackson was saying, because of what Thing was doing.

'Thing, *please* stop stroking my nose!' I asked it.

'But I *like* to. It is so big and *round*!' Thing purred.

Of course, Jackson started sniggering.

'Jackson, *don't*!' I hissed, hoping I wouldn't feel a tell-tale shudder from Thing.

Jackson mouthed an 'oops', then put on his best thoughtful face.

'Hey, *I* know! Maybe we could raid all the recycling bins in the estate!' he suggested. 'We're *bound* to find bits we could use to make a new shelter!'

'I like my *old* house. It is a *nice* house,' purred Thing, gently pressing the end of my nose, as if it might make a honking horn sound.

'It *was* a nice house,' I corrected it gently.

Poor Thing must have had to move again and again as the wreckers moved on and on, and the woods got steadily smaller and smaller. Till it finally ended up here, far away from wherever home used to be.

'Maybe old house still there, out past buildingings, in middle of woods . . .' said Thing, one paw still clutching my nose, the other pointing out past the foliage at the paved road beyond.

'But, Thing,' I sighed, leaning backwards to get my nose out of squidging distance, 'you *know* that's not true. There are no woods any more. And no house either.'

Thing's peaceful, leafy nest–or–whatever was now probably the site of a four-bedroom family home, complete with a whirling washing machine, blaring Wii games and screaming, dribbly toddlers.

'You know something else? Now I think of

it, one of those recycling *BINS* could make a great shelter!' Jackson exclaimed. 'It would be rainproof, and we'd just have to somehow cut a doorway in the side and—'

'Really, really, really want to see *old* house, Rubby,' Thing purred sadly and pointlessly, its giant eyes wide and forlorn. 'Really, really, really, really, *really* want to see old house.'

'I know you do,' I muttered sadly, ruffling the fur between its squirrelly ears. 'But—'

'D'you think someone would have a spare recycling bin they're not using?' Jackson interrupted, still full of plans for home improvements.

'And what will you say?' I laughed. '"Excuse me, but we need your bin for this weird talking creature we've got hidden away?"'

'"Course not!' Jackson replied. 'I'm not *that* stupid! I'd never let anything happen to . . . uh-oh! Where's Thing gone?'

ARRGHH!

In the blink of a (human) eye, Thing had scuttled off through the undergrowth.

'Oh no! It really *has* gone to find where its home used to be!' I blurted out.

'Quick, Ruby!' said Jackson, scrabbling to his feet. 'We've got to stop it — it'll get frightened! *And* it'll get seen by someone in one of the new houses!'

Worse than that, Thing might get cross when it got to where its home used to be, and found an ugly big building(ing) instead.

And if Thing got cross, it might do some magic.

And if Thing did some magic, we might really be in trouble.

I mean, really, really, really, really, *really* be in trouble…

9

Another ARRGHH!

Way back at the beginning of my story, I promised to tell you about Thing and Jackson and the jelly babies.

Oh, and the magic too.

So that's everything – right?

Not quite.

We're missing a little something: a curse.

Do you want to know about that? Are you sure?

'Cause it's coming (along with some more

magic!) and it nearly made me *sick* . . .

'Where is it?' said Jackson urgently, as we burst out of the trees and shrubs and on to Willow Avenue.

'You mean Thing? Or what used to be the middle of Muir Wood?' I asked, starting to run as fast as my flip-flops would let me.

(Which is not very fast, actually. If you've never tried it, don't – it's like trying to jog with pitta bread taped to your feet.)

'Both!' yelped Jackson.

'It's hard to tell,' I replied, fretting about the

way the new roads twisted and turned. They were taking us two steps forward and one step back from where we needed to be.

'Thing will have gone in a straight line, through people's gardens, won't it?' Jackson panted alongside me.

I didn't answer, because I was too busy concentrating on where we were going.

Plus I didn't want to stop and think about Thing being terrorised by fearsome dogs or startled gardeners with big, worrisome spades in their hands . . .

As we hurried towards a junction, I heard a noise that made my blood turn to ice.

'WAAAAAAAAHHHHHHHH!!'

I froze on the spot.

Jackson clunked into the back of me.

'What was that?' Jackson asked breathlessly.

I was pretty sure it was my worst nightmare.

Someone had spotted
Thing and screamed.
Thing was probably
scared stupid, and just
about to scream too.

Then there'd be lots *more*
screaming, and people rushing out of their
houses to see what the screaming was about.

Any minute now there'd be sirens and
police and scientists and people with stun
guns and big nets swarming all over the
place and it would be a total *disaster*!!

'Quick!' I yelped, grabbing hold of Jackson
by the T-shirt and pulling him after me.

'WAAAAAAAAHHHHHHHH!!'

We hurtled a few metres forward and saw . . .

A mum pushing a buggy at top speed out of a cul-de-sac.

The mum looked hassled and grumpy.

The little boy in the buggy was squiggling round – red-faced – and pointing back towards the semi-circle of identical houses behind him.

'MUMMMMEEEEE! STOP!!! WANNA CUDDLE THE NICE PUSSY!!!!!' he roared, bucking against the straps that held him in.

'*Oscar!*' the mum snapped. 'I said *no*! We're late for your junior gym class!'

'BUT I WANNA CUDDLE THE NICE PUSSY!!!!'

'I *said* no, Oscar!' the mum snapped again, stomping past me and Jackson as if we were invisible. 'Anyway, we don't know that cat and it might scratch you or have fleas or something nasty!'

'BUT THE NICE PUSSYYYYYYYY!!!'
wailed Oscar, his whole body twisted round,
his arms outstretched, his mum ignoring him
and hurtling off down the road and round
the corner.

'Hey, Ruby; check out the pussy!' said
Jackson.

'Huh?' I muttered, my ears still ringing
with distant 'WAAAAAHHHHHHHH!!'s.

'The pussy cat the kid wanted to cuddle –
it's over on the doormat of No. 72!'

Well, I guess that from a distance, a
passerby (or mum and whiny toddler) *might*
think the creature was a small, fuzzy ginger
cat, waiting patiently for its owner to come
home and give it its tea.

Unless they looked a little closer and saw
the squirrelly ears and the stumpy wings . . .

'Thing!' I called out, and flip-flapped

mighty fast towards our little buddy, with
Jackson sprinting past me. (Trainers beat
flip-flops every time.)

But Thing didn't answer – it was staring
hard at the front door of No. 72.

I glanced around, checking no one *else*
was about. Luckily, the pavements were
empty, the driveways had no cars parked in
them and the windows of the houses were all
shut tight.

But people would be drifting back from

school and work soon, surely.

We had to get Thing safely out of sight before anyone *else* appeared!

'What are you doing?' gasped Jackson, reaching Thing before me and flopping down beside it.

Thing still didn't say a purry word.

'Is this where your old home was?' I asked it, coming to a stop and bending over to get my breath back.

As I spoke, I noticed something I wished I hadn't.

Thing was *trembling*.

Its stumpy wings were *vibrating* ever-so-slightly.

'Jackson!' I said in alarm. 'It's feeling ARRGHH! Quick – have you got a jelly baby to distract it?'

Jackson began quickly rifling in his pockets, but it was too late.

The seriously spectacular weirdness had started . . .

CRACKLE

SPIT

FIZZZZzzZ!!

Flickers of light danced around the whole
of the front of the house.

Sparkles cartwheeled around the windows
and the door.

And then just as soon as the amazing mini
fireworks show started, it stopped.

'Thing – what did you *do*?!?' I asked all
a-tremble myself.

'I do a *curse*!' Thing purred darkly,
wobbling round to face me and Jackson.
'I send a giant cloud of *wasps* to live in this
house, where *my* house used to be!'

A giant cloud of wasps? I fretted to myself. *That sounds nasty!!*

'Um ...' mumbled Jackson.

He was pointing at something.

The letter box – it was creaking open slowly, as if it was being pushed from the inside.

EEK!

Were there *so* many wasps inside that they were squeezing their way out?!?

PLOP!

PLOP! PLOP! PLOP!

Jelly babies.

Instead of spiky, swarmy wasps, a whole bunch of brightly coloured jelly babies drop-drop-dropped on to the doormat.

'Thing . . . did your magic go a little bit *wrong*, like last time?' I asked, taking a couple of steps backwards and looking up at the windows.

Uh-oh.

'Peh,' said Thing, staring down at the yellow jelly baby at its feet.

'Wow!!' said Jackson, only just spotting what I had.

Squashed against the glass of every window in the house were multicoloured jelly babies.

There had to be hundreds; no, thousands; no, *millions* of jelly babies in there!

'The people who own this place are going to go *nuts* if they see this!' I garbled. 'They'll phone the police and the newspapers and heaps of people will come down to see and Thing might get discovered and WHAT ARE WE GOING TO DO?!'

Before Jackson had a chance to answer, a terrible sound made me go rigid.

PLINKY-PLINK! A-PLINKY-PLINK! PLINK-PLINK-PLINK-PLINK!!

'Oh, no . . . *please* don't let the driver see us!' I murmured, watching as an ice-cream van cruised up to the junction, some nursery rhyme trilling loudly from a speaker.

'Of *course* he'll see us! It's like ice-cream van drivers have a special radar to spot kids!'

Jackson was right; the van had now turned into

the cul-de-sac, and was gliding straight towards us.

Help . . .

'Wait; Dad gave me my pocket money this morning,' said Jackson, jumping to his feet and jangling some coins in his pocket. 'I'll go and head him off.'

With that, Jackson bolted down the drive, along the pavement and made the van pull up outside No. 64.

'Quick, Thing – act like a cat!' I ordered, as I crouched in front of the door, so that the jelly babies dropping from the letter box were hidden from view. (If the ice-cream man spotted the ones in the windows, he might think they were just some crazy style of curtains. Hopefully.)

'What is *scat*?' asked Thing, rubbing his paws together anxiously.

'Like . . . like Christine! You know; the old

furry animal in my bedroom?' I explained urgently.

'Oh! Yes!' said Thing, immediately curling into a ball and closing its eyes.

As I stroked the 'cat' with a shaking hand, I saw Jackson being handed a large cone.

Then with a big fake smile, he waved as the ice-cream man got back behind the wheel and set off in search of more kid customers.

'It's OK – the van is going now,' I whispered to Thing, who stayed curled up. Curled up and *snoring*.

Good grief; it had actually fallen asleep!

'Thing! Wake *up*!' I urged, as Jackson hurried back towards us.

Thing dozily blinked its big eyes and gave a furry stretch, along with a mewling sort of yawn. It would have looked ever so cute, if there wasn't a complete *emergency* going on right behind us.

'This has given me an idea!' said Jackson, taking a lick of his ice-cream cone before chucking it into the nearest bush.

For a second, I felt relieved – till I remembered this was *Jackson* talking, and his idea was probably going to be *dumb*.

It was.

Get this . . .

Cupping his hands under the letter box, Jackson caught a bundle of tumbling jelly babies – then stuffed them in his mouth.

'Come on, *both* of you!' he mumbled and chewed. '*Eat*!!'

Yes, it was dumb, but because I couldn't think of anything better I did as I was told. (Thing began nervously nibbling too, glancing back and forth, from me to Jackson.)

But by my thirtieth jelly baby, I had

figured out a *new* plan – which was useful,
because I was starting to feel quite sick.

'Listen, Thing!' I began. 'You have GOT to
magic this away!'

'Sorry, sorry, *sorry* – can't magic the magic
away, Rubby!' Thing muttered, frantically
rubbing its paws together. 'I *scared* now . . .'

It felt scared?! Scared was no use. Thing
had to feel ARRGHH!, but how was *that*
going to happen?!?

Then I looked at Jackson, who gave me a

big baboon grin back with his cheeks jam-packed full of jelly babies.

'Jackson! Be annoying! NOW!!' I ordered him, knowing – out of all the annoying boys I'd ever met – that Jackson could do it.

'Huh?' he mumbled dopily.

Quickly, I clamped my hands over Thing's furry ears so it couldn't hear. 'We've *got* to make it cross! If it doesn't feel *ARRGHH!*, then we don't stand a chance!'

'Yeah, but how?' asked Jackson, with a massive, sugary gulp.

How annoying that Jackson didn't seem to know how to be annoying!

'Oh, for goodness sake, act like a *mean squirrel*!' I hissed at him.

Thing was scrambling at my hands, trying to set its ears free.

So I let go, hoping Jackson wouldn't let us all down.

'Er . . . ha ha ha!' he started lamely.

Thing didn't look so scared suddenly; just a little bit confused.

'Just look at yourself!' Jackson tried again. 'You've got those funny little wings – bet you can't even *fly*! Ha ha ha!!'

Thing still seemed confused, but started rocking from side to side.

'Hey, *I* know a good name for you!' said Jackson, getting going at last. '"Big-nose-no-tail"! Yeah, *that's* good!'

'Peh!' muttered Thing, clenching its tiny paws.

'Big-nose-no-tail! Big-nose-no-tail!' Jackson sing-songed.

As he carried on, I saw Thing start to tremble – great! But I needed it to concentrate and use all that *ARRGHH!* to change the spell on the house, *not* to turn Jackson into a cucumber or a wardrobe or something.

Scooping it up, I held Thing in front of the jellified living room window and said, 'Now—'

(The sound of distant crackles were already in the air.)

'—take the curse back quick—'

(The flickers of light began to dance.)

'—and reverse the magic—'

(CRACKLE -SPIT - FIZZZZZZZZ!!)

'—please!!'

(Sparkles cartwheeled all around us.)

As soon as the mini fireworks show started, it stopped.

And instead of a house packed with jelly babies, a peaceful empty building stood in front of us.

Well . . . not *quite*.

'Butterflies?!?' gasped Jackson, as millions of dainty coloured wings fluttered around inside.

'Sorry, sorry, *sorry*!' muttered Thing, twisting round to look up at me with its bushbaby eyes.

It was OK.

In that moment, I realised that same as Jackson was a friend who couldn't help being annoying, Thing had magical powers that happened to be *rubbish* . . .

But we were still left with a pretty big problem.

'How do we get *these* out?' I sighed, nodding at the butterflies, flittering around the light fittings and sofas.

'Ta *na*!' grinned Jackson, flipping open the letter box.

And sure enough, a butterfly quivered out.

Then another.

And another.

And a whole flittery-flutter of them.

And soon – well, fifteen minutes later, with both me and Jackson taking turns – they were all gone, dancing and prancing around the ugly Forest View Estate, making it an altogether prettier place to be.

'Right, Jackson; you, me and Thing need to go home,' I said, as the final pair of wings wibbled off in the wind. (And not a second too soon – a car was just turning into the cul-de-sac.)

'Yes, *please*,' purred Thing, from the safety of my hoodie top.

'And no more magic,' I warned it, folding my arms gently across my chest, to hide the Thing-shaped lump there.

'No, *thank* you,' it purred back, its hand coming up towards my face, offering me a half-chewed jelly baby only *slightly* covered in ginger hairs.

How sweet.

Not to mention *yucky* . . .

10

Once upon an end

What happened next?

(Or since it's the last chapter, should that be what happened *last*?)

Well, the day after the curse, me and Jackson both arrived at the trees after school with presents.

I got there first, with a handful of white, fat mushrooms snaffled from the vegetable compartment of our fridge.

'Ah!! So big round mushrooms, Rubby!'

gasped Thing. 'Where they been growed so big?'

'Er . . . the supermarket,' I answered, since I didn't have the packet to hand, to read which country they were from.

'Supermarket must be *nice* wood. No big round mushrooms like this in my *old* wood. You take me to Supermarket Wood sometime?'

Oh, dear, I could feel my head go twisty with explanations again.

Luckily, Jackson showed up right about then.

'Hi, guys!!' he said, swinging his legs over his tall garden fence and landing – *CRONK* – exactly on top of Thing's squint stick-and-bag home. The big donut.

'EEK!' squeaked Thing in shock.

'Jackson! Look what you've *done*!' I moaned.

'Oops! But it's OK! Honest!' Jackson babbled, pulling something out of a big bag in his hand. 'See what *I've* got!'

'It' was a large plastic toy van.

'So?' I muttered, wondering what Jackson was on about.

'*So* . . . it's a Scooby-Doo Mystery Machine!' Jackson explained, looking stunned that I hadn't recognised it straightaway. 'This used to be my *favourite* toy *ever*!'

'And what – you want us all to play with it now?' I teased him.

'No, course not!' grinned Jackson. 'Just check this out . . .'

He tugged the back doors of the van open.

Thing looked at me and I looked at Thing.

Nope, neither of us understood.

'A *perfect* snug and dry den for Thing to curl up in!' Jackson announced with a flourish of his arms.

Thing made a little surprised 'Hmmmff!' sound and peeked inside.

'I guess it *could* work,' I admitted. 'But we'll have to cover it up, so no one spots it . . .'

'Yes! We can park it *here*—'

Jackson drove the brightly coloured van into the nook of some tree roots. (I *swear* he was making *brum-brum* noises under his breath.)

'—and cover it with branches and moss and stuff!'

As he grabbed some greenery to disguise the Mystery Machine, Thing watched with great interest.

'What do you think?' Jackson asked it finally, brushing his blond hair back from his face and getting some moss stuck in it.

'It's nice . . .' Thing nodded, rubbing its
paws together nervously.

'You could put stuff inside, to make it
. . . um . . . *crunchy* like your old home!' I
suggested (even though I didn't know what I
was talking about).

'Yes! Yes, *please!*' Thing jabbered, now
clapping its paws together excitedly.

I glanced at Jackson, and smiled a you-
did-good smile at him.

Jackson looked chuffed and shy at the
same time, and hid his awkwardness by
sticking his hand under his arm and making

a *ffftt!* noise.

'Boy? Rubby?' we suddenly heard Thing say, and swirled round to see our tiny furry friend blinking up at us.

'Yes, Thing?' I said gently.

'Boy and Rubby very *nice* to me,' it purred, rocking from side to side, with its paws behind its back. 'Give me pressles.'

'Presents,' I corrected it under my breath, 'cause I didn't want to go and sound all teacherly, like Miss Wilson.

'So now I give *Boy* and *Rubby* pressles . . .'

And with a swoosh, one tiny paw came out and presented Jackson with a twig.

'Oh . . . *thank* you!' he grinned, practically choking a laugh back down. 'It's a very good stick!'

'It quite *twangy*,' said Thing, pinging the twig so it boinged a bit in Jackson's hand.

'Well, thanks. I do like them twangy,' Jackson replied, trying so hard not to snigger that I worried he might explode.

'And Rubby, is for *you* . . .'

Thing's other paw came from behind its back, clutching a newly-yanked-from-the-ground clump of grass.

'I pick them myself!' it said.

'That's *so* sweet!' I replied, taking the grass, and ever-so-gently shaking the earth off the bottom.

'I *remember* you like to keep them in bottle

till they deaded!' Thing smiled happily at me, proud of how well it had done with its pressles.

'Yes, that's true,' I nodded, thinking I might just explode with giggles too.

'Peh! I got OTHER pressle for Rubby!!' Thing suddenly exclaimed, and ran off to rummage under some damp leaves.

At first, I didn't recognise the grubby, uneven ball it scampered back to offer to me.

'Pretty Rubby wrapping!' Thing blinked cutely at me.

I took a hold of whatever it was and gave it a shake – and my muddy, daisy-print pants unfurled about ten centimetres from Jackson's nose ...

And to finish my story, I am going to tell you three lies:

- I wasn't at all embarrassed about the pants

- Jackson **didn't** burst out laughing at me, and . . .

- Thing **never** did magic again

Ha!

Coming soon . . .

you, me and Thing

The Dreaded Noodle-Doodles

Thing stays safe and hidden at the bottom of the garden.

Well, *most* of the time.

But last week we snuck it into school (bad move).

And thanks to Thing and its rubbish magic, we ended up in a totally noodly, doodly mess!

Gulp . . .